I Hate Everyone

To Rosie, who makes the world a friendlier place –
M.K.

To my daughter, Kate –
R.P.

First published in the United Kingdom in 2002 by David Bennett Books Limited.

Text copyright © 2002 Mij Kelly.
Illustrations copyright © 2002 Ruth Palmer.

BRITISH LIBRARY CATALOGUING-IN-PUBLICATION DATA
A catalogue record for this book is available from the British Library.

ISBN 1 85602 362 1
Printed and bound in China

I Hate Everyone

Written by

Mij Kelly

Illustrated by

Ruth Palmer

DAVID BENNETT BOOKS

Queen Bee leapt out of bed.
"Fetch my clothes and my crown," she said.

But her chambermaids just frowned
and stood around. They folded
their arms. They shook their heads.

"Look here,
Queen Bee," they said.
"You don't have to
beg or get down on
your knees, but you
could at least
say **please.**"

"Why should I?"
Queen Bee scoffed and stomped off.

"I'm not using this!" Queen Bee hissed.
"Fetch me something nice.
Fetch me the toothpaste
that tastes of strawberry ice."

But the lady of the bath tub said
'tut tut tut' like a dripping tap.
"You can't speak to me like
that! No way, Queen Bee.
I shan't fetch your
toothpaste until
you say **please.**"

"Oh get lost!"
said Queen Bee
and flounced off.

"I want a boiled egg, buttered toast and tea," said Queen Bee.
"Plus ice cream with hot toffee sauce, of course, and blueberry muffins, huckleberry pies..."

Queen Bee rolled her eyes.
"And, oh yes, I almost forgot, a big chocolate cake with cherries on top!"

"Is that the lot?" the cook growled.
"I think not!"

"You see, Queen Bee, I shan't make your breakfast until you say **please.**"

"Oh go and boil your head!"
Queen Bee said. She was so annoyed
her face turned red. She was so annoyed
she almost went back to bed.
But she stormed off to the dining room instead.

"Pour me a cup of tea!"
yelled Queen Bee.

"Are you talking to me?"
the butler said. He raised his
black bushy eyebrows
and sadly shook
his head.

"I'm sorry,
Queen Bee...

...but I shan't
pour your tea
until you say **please.**"

"Stop picking on me!"
Queen Bee roared.

She was so upset and sore that she stormed
out the front door. She stamped on the
daisies and kicked up the dirt.
She felt hurt.

But she was the Queen.

She'd make them all sorry for being so mean.

"Arrest them all!"

Queen Bee blustered.

Her secretary looked really flustered.

"Put everyone in jail.

Do it at once, you snot-headed snail!"

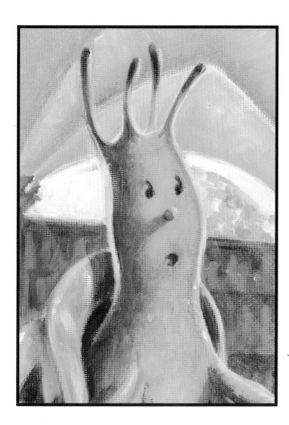

"I can't do that, Queen Bee," said her secretary. "And besides, we've all agreed that we're not going to help you unless you say **please.**"

"You're all being mean!" screamed the Queen. She stamped her feet.

She stuck our her tongue.

"I hate everyone!"

she roared like thunder.

Then off she blundered
down
the steep
dark steps
that led

underground...

...and there she found
a deep dark dungeon.

She locked herself in
and threw away the key.

Queen Bee felt fizzing mad. She felt sad.
And the sadness she felt was so big and
so bad that it came bursting out of her eyes.
"Why is everyone so
horrible?" she cried.
"Nobody loves me.
I've lost all my friends.
I've come to a lonely, miserable end.

And the worst of it is,"
Queen Bee wailed,
"I've gone and
locked myself
in jail."

"No you haven't," someone said.

Queen Bee raised her head.

"I need a hug and a squeeze," she said.

"Please."

"Yippee Queen Bee!
See, please is like
a hug and a squeeze
or the smile on your face."